Farmer Skiboo Stories

Martin Waddell

Illustrated by
Julie Fletcher

dingles & company

First published in the United States of America in 2008 by
dingles & company
P.O. Box 508
Sea Girt, New Jersey 08750

First Printing

Website: www.dingles.com
E-mail: info@dingles.com

Library of Congress Catalog Card Number
2007906276

ISBN
978-1-59646-886-3 (library binding)
978-1-59646-887-0 (paperback)

Farmer Skiboo Stories
Text © Martin Waddell, 2002
This U.S. edition of *Farmer Skiboo Stories*, originally published in
English in 2007, is published by arrangement with
Oxford University Press.

The moral rights of the author have been asserted.
Database right Oxford University Press (maker).

Printed in China

Contents

Cock-a-doodle-doo

It was midnight,
and the farmyard was still.
The full moon rose over the hill.
It flooded the farm with its light.

"I think I'll play a trick on Farmer
Skiboo," thought Barn Owl.

He went, *"Too-wit-too-woooo,"* very softly.
It was just loud enough to wake up the
Silly Old Rooster.

"What's this?" thought Silly Old
Rooster. "I'm awake. It must be dawn."
He went, *"Cock-a-doodle-doo,"*
to wake up the rest of the farm.
Cock-a-doodle-doo

The cows in the field heard
Silly Old Rooster calling.
They thought it must be morning.

"It's milking time," thought the cows.
"There goes the Rooster!"

And they went, "*Moo-moo-moo-mooo*,"
calling for someone to milk them.

Cock-a-doodle-doo

Moo-moo-moo-mooo

Brown Hen was asleep in the hedges.
The noise woke her up.

"There goes the Rooster.
It must be time for my egg," she said.

She laid one at once.
And she went, *"Cluck-cluck-cluck-cluck,"*
because she was so pleased with
the egg she had laid.

Cock-a-doodle-doo
Moo-moo-moo-mooo
Cluck-cluck-cluck-cluck

The ducks and the ducklings were down by the pond.

"He's done it again. That Silly Old Rooster has wakened Brown Hen!" they decided. "It must be time for our swim."

They all waddled in for their swim.

And the ducks and ducklings went,
"Quack-quack-quack-quack,"
the way all ducks do,
when the water is cold in the morning.

Cock-a-doodle-doo
Moo-moo-moo-mooo
Cluck-cluck-cluck-cluck
Quack-quack-quack-quack

Faithful Dog Tom was asleep
in the farmer's armchair.
He was too old to sleep out of doors.
    "There goes Silly Old Rooster.
It must be get-up-and-do time
for the farmer and me!" he thought.

Faithful Dog Tom padded upstairs.
He pushed open the door of the
farmer's bedroom.

And he barked,
"Bow-wow-wow-woooooo,"
to wake up Farmer Skiboo.

Cock-a-doodle-doo
Moo-moo-moo-mooo
Cluck-cluck-cluck-cluck
Quack-quack-quack-quack
Bow-wow-wow-woooooo

Farmer Skiboo was in bed.
The barking woke him up.
   He climbed out of bed
without waking Mrs. Skiboo.
He yawned and scratched.
He put on his boots and his hat.
He pulled back the curtains
to let in the light of the morning.

Farmer Skiboo saw the moon
shining bright.

"OO-OO-OO-OO-OOOH!"
moaned Farmer Skiboo.

Cock-a-doodle-doo
Moo-moo-moo-mooo
Cluck-cluck-cluck-cluck
Quack-quack-quack-quack
Bow-wow-wow-woooooo
OO-OO-OO-OO-OOOH!

14

The moon shone down on
    Silly Old Rooster crowing,
    the cows who were mooing,
    Brown Hen and her egg,
    the cold ducks who swam on the pond,
    Faithful Dog Tom,
    and Farmer Skiboo.
    "STOP THAT NOISE!
GET BACK TO BED!" yelled Farmer Skiboo.
He was dancing and prancing with rage.

He took off his boot
and chucked it at Silly Old Rooster.
CRASH-BANG-SMACK-WALLOP-YAROOO!

Cock-a-doodle-doo
Moo-moo-moo-mooo
Cluck-cluck-cluck-cluck
Bow-wow-wow-woooooo
OO-OO-OO-OO-OOOH!
STOP-THAT-NOISE!
GET-BACK-TO-BED!
CRASH-BANG-SMACK-WALLOP-
YAROOO!

All the noise stopped at once.

The farmyard was peaceful and quiet
and still. The animals went back to sleep.

The only sound was the squeak
of the springs as Farmer Skiboo
climbed into bed.

And then …

Someone called,

"*Too-wit-too-woooo,*" very softly.

It was just loud enough to waken
Silly Old Rooster and …

Cock-a-doodle-doo
Moo-moo-moo-mooo
Cluck-cluck-cluck-cluck
Quack-quack-quack-quack
Bow-wow-wow-woooooo
OO-OO-OO-OO-OOOH!
STOP-THAT-NOISE!
GET-BACK-TO-BED!
CRASH-BANG-SMACK-WALLOP-
YAROOOOOO!

Four Fools in a Field

Chapter 1

A Problem for Charlie

Farmer Skiboo called Charlie to help with the bull.

Charlie looked at the bull.

The bull looked at Charlie.

The bull didn't think much of Charlie.

"Get the bull out of this field, Charlie," said Farmer Skiboo. "But don't wreck my hedge when you do it!"

"Right!" said Charlie.

Charlie looked at the bull and the hedge.
The hedge was very small.
The bull was a whole lot of bull.

How could Charlie
get the bull over the hedge?
He didn't know.

"Well, here goes, I suppose!"
Charlie said.

He crawled in under the bull.

The bull looked in under himself.

He saw Charlie there …

He still didn't think much
of Charlie.

Charlie tried to stand up.

He had the bull on his back.

He was trying to lift the bull over the hedge.

Charlie puffed and he pulled.

He couldn't budge the old bull.

"Ned!" Charlie said. "Give me a hand with this bull."

Ned took one end of the bull.

Charlie stood at the other.

They puffed and they pulled.

They still couldn't budge the old bull.

"Send for Bert and Sid," Ned told Charlie.

Bert and Sid came, and they each took
one of the bull's legs.

"ONE, TWO, THREE, LIFT."

And they puffed and they pulled,
but they couldn't budge that old bull.

Chapter 2
Stuck with the Bull!

They sat down to think.

The four fools looked at the bull.

The bull looked at the fools.

The bull didn't think much of the fools.

"We could dig a bull
tunnel, under the
hedge," Charlie said.

Nobody wanted to dig.
"We're stuck with that bull!"
Charlie said.

28

Chapter 3

Small Anne to the Rescue!

Along came Farmer Skiboo's daughter, Small Anne.

"I know how to do it!" she said.

Small Anne opened the gate.

She LED the bull out of the field, without touching the hedge.

She closed the gate.

She patted the bull on the head.

Then Small Anne walked away whistling.

Ned, Bert, and Sid beamed at the bull. But Charlie stood scratching his head.

"What if Farmer Skiboo wants that bull BACK in the field?" Charlie said. "How can we put the bull back without busting the hedge?"

"I dunno …" sighed Ned.

"Me neither!" sobbed Bert.

"Forget it!" said Sid.

Then …

"GOT IT!" Charlie said. "If he wants the bull back in the field, we just send for Small Anne."

And that's what they did.

About the author

I have been trying to get Farmer Skiboo into a story for ages. Why? Because I like the way the words work together. A farmer with a name like "Skiboo" sounded interesting to work on. So I needed a farm story. Skiboo... and cock-a-doodle-doo... do you see what I mean about the sound of the words?

The best stories often begin that way.